KAREN POPHAM took a Fine Arts degree at Central St. Martins then went on to teach at Colchester Art College and Lewisham Art College. She has been artist in residence at the Reform Club and the Laban Centre and has exhibited at the Royal Academy and the Royal Festival Hall. Karen has written and illustrated the *Little Swan* series for Random House. She lives in London with her husband and three children, two of whom are the William and Ellie of the story.

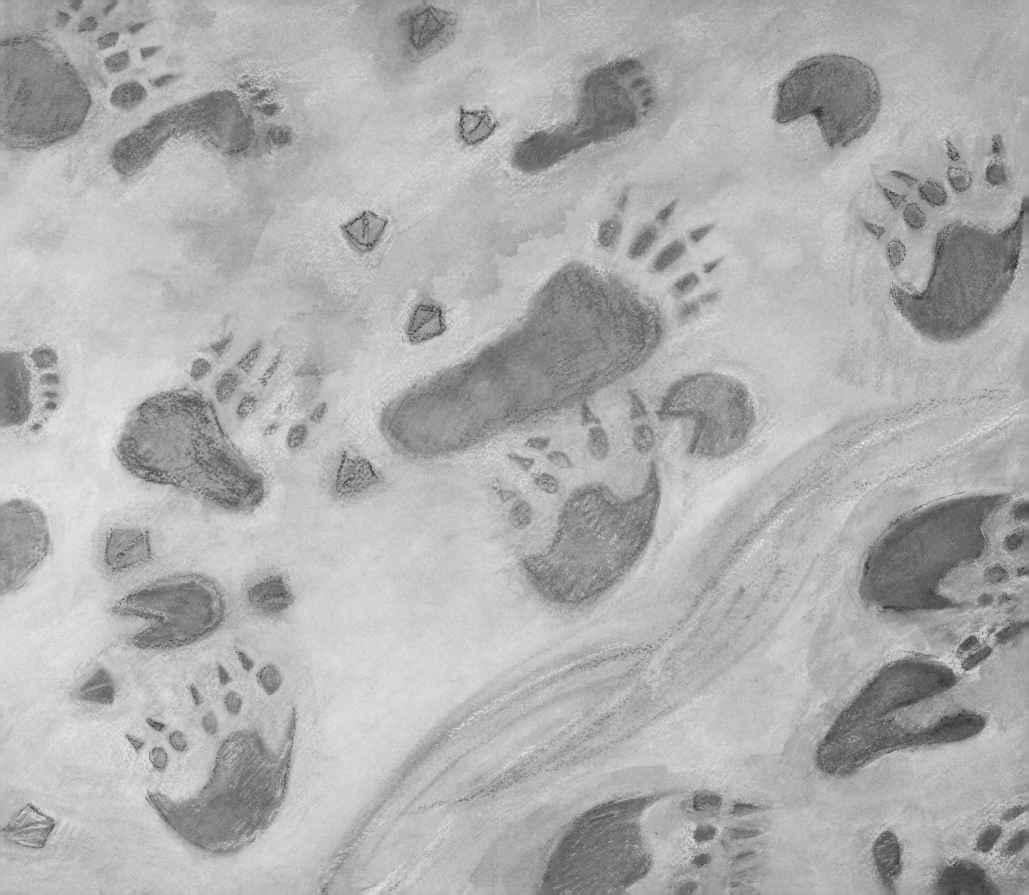

Ellie's growl copyright © Frances Lincoln Limited 2000
Text and illustrations copyright © Karen Popham 2000

First published in Great Britain in 2000 by
Frances Lincoln Limited, 4 Torriano Mews,
Torriano Avenue, London NW5 2RZ

First paperback edition 2001

British Library Cataloguing in Publication Data
available on request

ISBN 0-7112-1504-9 hardback
ISBN 0-7112-1505-7 paperback

Printed in Hong Kong

3 5 7 9 8 6 4 2

Ellie's growl

Karen Popham

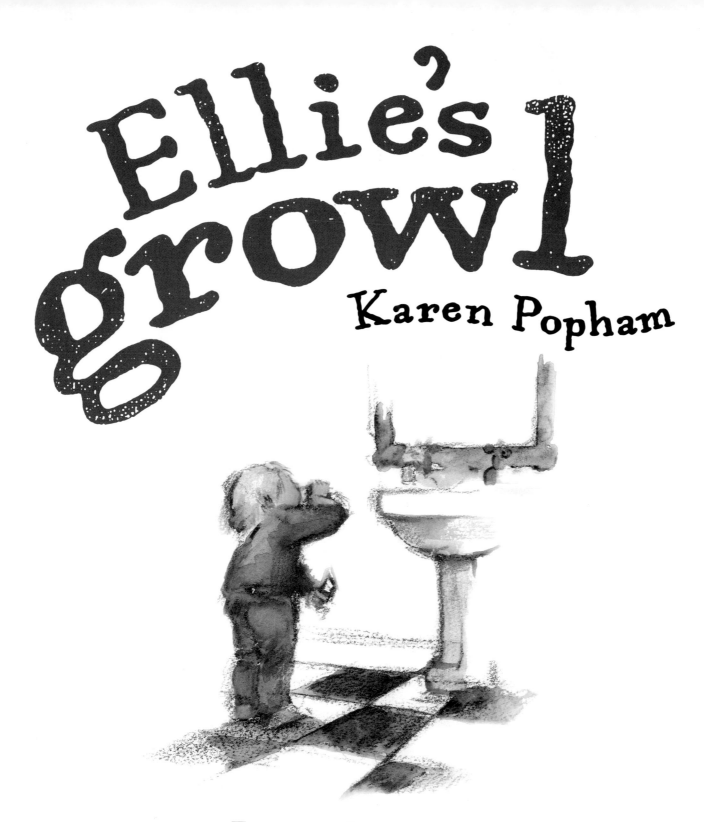

FRANCES LINCOLN

For Christopher — K.P.

Ellie likes her bedtime books, especially stories about animals. She likes it best of all when her big brother William reads them to her, because he makes wonderful animal noises.

William can make the sound sea lions make when they **challenge** each other.

He can **flap** and **spit** like an angry swan,

whinny like zebras jumping,

and
croak
like courting toads.

William **blusters** like

polar bears swimming,

he can **ssss** like a snake when it's slithering,

and **beat** his chest like a baboon does...

...when it's in the mood.

He can even **sing** like
the great blue whale.

One evening William reads
Ellie a jungle story.
And when the tiger prowls...

...William **growlS!**

Next morning, while she is cleaning her teeth,

Ellie likes growling.

After breakfast she **growls** at the dog.

The dog hides.

After lunch she **growls** at a little boy.

The boy howls.

After tea she **growls** at a cow.
The cow walks away.

At bath-time Ellie **growls** at William.

William gets cross.

At bedtime
she **growls**
at the kitten.
But the kitten...

...growl**S** back!

Ellie cries.

   The kitten comes and nuzzles her and begins to purr. Ellie listens carefully, then she tries to purr too,

and William comes in...

...to read them both a story.

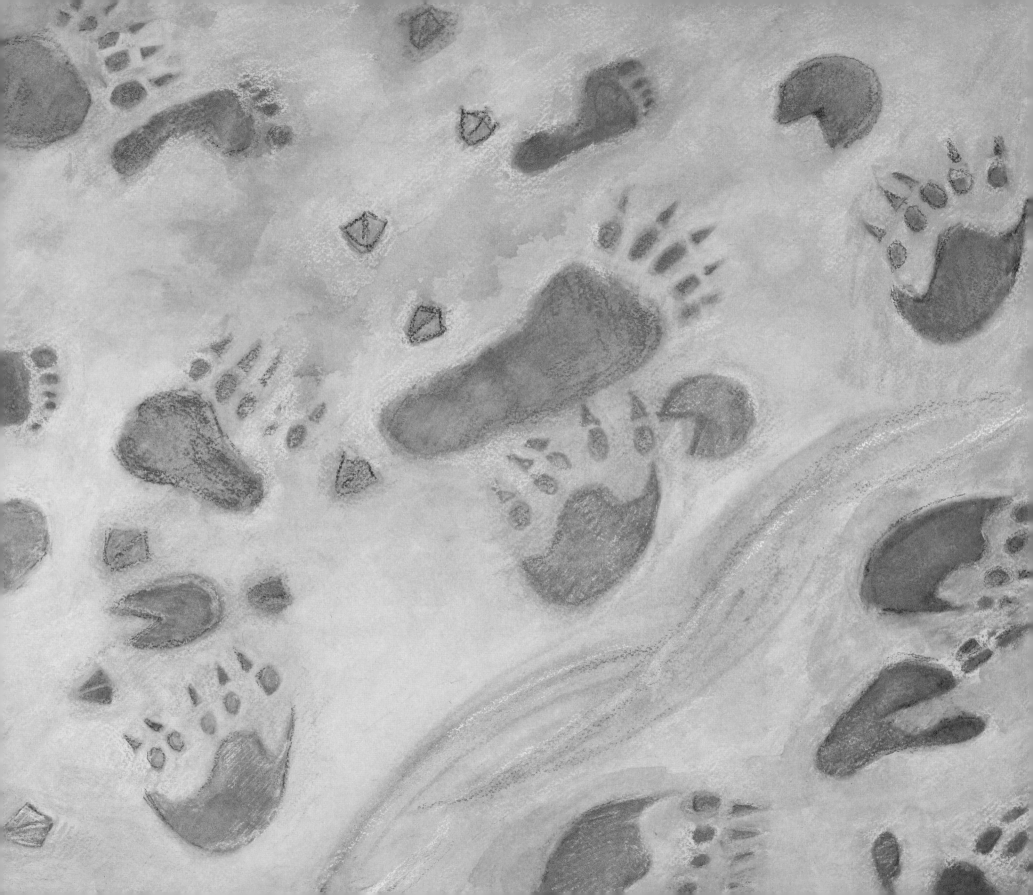

MORE PAPERBACKS AVAILABLE FROM FRANCES LINCOLN

Copy Me, Copycub
Richard Edwards
Illustrated by **Susan Winter**

Everything his mother does, Copycub does too; splashing through streams, picking berries and climbing trees to find honey. But one freezing winter's day, Copycub is too tired to follow his mother, even though his life depends on it...

Suitable for Early Years Education and for National Curriculum English – Reading, Key Stage 1
Scottish Guidelines English Language – Reading, Level A
ISBN 0-7112-1460-3

Simply Delicious!
Margaret Mahy
Illustrated by **Jonathan Allen**

Mr Minky has bought a double-dip-chocolate-chip-and-cherry ice cream with rainbow twinkles and chopped-nut sprinkles. But to get it home he has to cycle through the jungle, and all the animals want a taste...

Suitable for National Curriculum English – Reading, Key Stage 1
Scottish Guidelines English Language – Reading, Levels A and B
ISBN 0-7112-1441-7

The Mouse and the Apple
Stephen Butler

Mouse longs for the ripe red apple hanging on the apple tree. The other animals have their eyes on it, too – but how can they get it down?

Suitable for National Curriculum English – Reading, Key Stage 1
Scottish Guidelines English Language – Reading, Level A
ISBN 0-7112-0856-5

Frances Lincoln titles are available from all good bookshops.